A Perfect Snowman

For my beautiful wife,
Cindy, and my daughters,
Abby and Liz

SIMON & SCHUSTER BOOKS FOR YOUNG READERS

An imprint of Simon & Schuster Children's Publishing Division

1230 Avenue of the Americas, New York, New York 10020

Copyright © 2007 by Preston McDaniels

All rights reserved, including the right of reproduction in whole or in part in any form.

SIMON & SCHUSTER BOOKS FOR YOUNG READERS is a trademark of Simon & Schuster, Inc.

Book design by Daniel Roode

The text for this book is set in Cochin.

The illustrations for this book are rendered in blended graphite.

Manufactured in China

6 8 10 9 7 5

CIP data for this book is available from the Library of Congress.

ISBN-13: 978-1-4169-1026-8

ISBN-10: 1-4169-1026-3

A Perfect Snowman

WRITTEN AND ILLUSTRATED BY

PRESTON McDANIELS

SIMON & SCHUSTER BOOKS FOR YOUNG READERS
New York   London   Toronto   Sydney

There once was a boy who lived in a very large house with very high walls all around it. He wore the finest clothes and went to the finest school, and each night he sat himself down to a perfectly fine dinner before going off to bed.

One winter morning the boy awoke to find the world outside his window covered with newly fallen snow. It was a wonderfully wet and heavy snow, the sort that was perfect for making things like a snowman, which was just what the boy decided he would do.

So he put on his coat and his cap and hurried downstairs to find the things he needed. He fetched the finest carrot from the kitchen and several perfectly round lumps of coal from the cellar. And when no one was looking, he took his father's finest hat, favorite scarf, and best umbrella from the hall.

Then he stepped out into the cold morning air to begin building

a perfect snowman.

He began by rolling three perfectly round balls, each one slightly larger than the one before. Then he found two perfectly strong sticks from the oak tree that grew straight and tall outside his window and used them for arms.

When he was finished, it was plain for all to see that this was the *finest* snowman a small boy had ever made. Neighborhood children peeked over the walls to see it, and people passing on the street stopped by to say how truly remarkable it was.

All the while the snowman just stood, quietly listening to the kind things they said about him. And the more he listened, the more he came to believe that what they said was true.

So it went on for hours that wonderful wintry day.

But even the best of times must eventually come to an end, and the boy was called in to supper.

The snowman slowly looked about, curious to see if there was anyone left to admire him. But all he saw was the warm glow of lights shining through the windows as the world around him began to settle down for the long night.

Standing alone in the darkness, the snowman waited for the young boy to come back outside. But the cold night deepened and darkened, and the boy did not return. There were no giggling children to peek over the walls, and not a single soul passing by on the street. The only things in sight were an old rabbit and her children, sniffing about in the snow-covered garden.

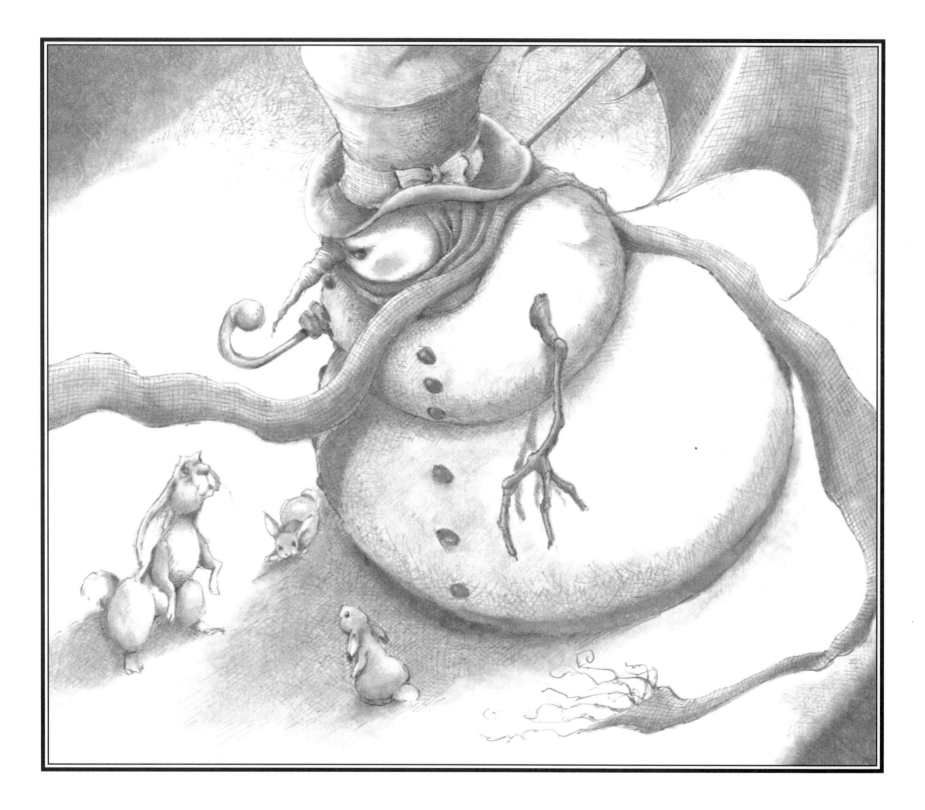

At first, the rabbit didn't know what to think of the snowman, so she kept herself at a safe distance. But, when she noticed the handsome carrot in the middle of his face, she became quite excited and crept closer.

"Pardon me," she said, "but would you mind sharing some of that old carrot with me and my children?"

The snowman grew angry at the rabbit for saying such a terrible thing. "That *old* carrot just happens to be my nose," he snarled. "And it's a very fine nose at that!"

"Oh, I beg your pardon," squeaked the rabbit, feeling rather ashamed for what she had said. "Why, I certainly didn't mean to offend you . . . it's just that, well . . . there is nothing to eat."

The snowman, nearly trembling with rage, roared, "So you thought you might as well come begging for my beautiful nose?"

"Please, kind sir, it's nothing like that at all," wept the rabbit. "It's not for me that I beg but for my children. They are so cold and haven't had a scrap of food for who knows how long."

The snowman looked down at the rabbit's shivering brood and, for just a moment, felt his icy heart begin to thaw.

"I *suppose* I would still be nearly perfect without my nose," he thought. So he reluctantly plucked the carrot from his face and placed it on the tiny paws before him.

The grateful rabbit and her children fled into the shadows with their treasure, leaving the snowman behind to rub the empty place where he once had a nose.

"Such wretched little creatures," he muttered. "I suppose it comes from not being perfect."

Then he settled himself down again, waiting for the boy to return and make things better.

Several hours had passed

and the boy was nowhere in sight. Along

the street, one by one, the warm glow disappeared

from windows, and clouds began to cover the moon.

The snowman was beginning to feel quite alone and

altogether forgotten, but still thought himself very much

perfect, when a cat came wandering along the garden wall

and stopped by for a visit.

"This night's not fit for man nor beast, is it?" said the cat.

"I really don't mind it so much," replied the snowman,

then he looked away. He thought it was rather beneath

him to discuss the weather with a neighborhood stray.

"No, I suppose you wouldn't," said the cat with a sigh. "This bitter cold seems to be your cup of tea, but it's nearly more than I can bear. Would it be too much to ask if I may borrow your hat and scarf?"

The snowman laughed at the cat for asking such a foolish question.

"Why would I want to give *you* these fine things that I wear so well? A sorry creature like you would most likely spoil them with fleas or lose them chasing some rat down an alley."

The cat hung its head and sighed. "It's true that I'm not perfect. I have never known an evening fire or a kind lap or a bowl of warm milk at the end of the day. But I do what I must to get by in this world, so won't you please show me some pity?"

The snowman looked the old cat over carefully. His hair was thin and his body was scarred and shivering from the cold. Once again the snowman felt his icy heart melt just a little, and he removed his hat and scarf and gave them to the cat.

The snowman watched the cat disappear into the darkness
and began to wonder how much worse things could be. All
that was left of him now were three balls of snow, several
lumps of coal, and an umbrella. Worst of all, he was
beginning to wonder if the boy would ever come
back to make things better.

Snow began to fall over the sleeping

town. In the beginning it fell softly, but in time,

it grew into a wicked storm. The tall branches

creaked and cracked and thrashed back and forth,

desperately trying to stand against the bitter wind.

Through it all the snowman waited for the boy to

return. But with each lonely passing hour the

snowman's once-melting heart grew colder again.

He hated himself for taking pity on the rabbits

and the cat, and he wished he could take every-

thing back so that he could be perfect once again.

Quite to his surprise, he heard a tiny voice

call out of the darkness. "Excuse me, sir.

May I please have a piece of coal?"

Before him stood an angelic little girl, who seemed to appear out of nowhere, all alone and dressed in tatters. Her feet were wrapped in rags, and her lips quivered from the cold. Her face was beautiful but as pale as the snow. She looked up at the snowman and spoke again. "Please, Mr. Snowman, I am *so* cold. May I please have some of your coals to keep me warm?"

Just then something remarkable happened. For one shining moment the snowman forgot about the rabbits that ate his nose, the cat who wore his clothes, and how perfect he had once been.

He forgot about himself altogether and bowed slowly before the little girl, allowing the lumps of coal to fall, one by one, into her waiting apron. He then handed her his umbrella to keep off the wind and snow.

The angelic little girl hugged and kissed him and softly whispered, "Oh, thank you, dear sir. Your kindness will *never* be forgotten."

She turned away, as if for the last time, and vanished into the storm.

The next morning came, and then another, but the boy never returned to make things better, and the little girl never appeared again.

One bright morning the sun rose and woke the trees, the grass, and the flowers, telling them winter was over and the time had finally come to grow again.

The air was filled with the sweet smells of spring, but the snowman had already begun to melt away into a puddle.

The sun took the puddle, drop by drop,
far above the large house with high walls all
around it, to a place where the air was cold
and clear and the stars shone brightly.

There, the snowman woke to a wondrous sight.

Before him was the little girl dressed in tatters, her face as pure and beautiful as newly fallen snow.

She smiled at him sweetly and said, "Hello, Mr. Snowman. I have been waiting for you for a very long time. Won't you please come stay with me?"

And so he remained there with her, together forever . . .

just the two of them, as perfectly happy as they could be.